Journey to the
Far Islands

Sandra Waggoner

Sable Creek
PRESS

Glendale, Arizona

ISBN 9780989066761

Printed in the United States of America
First Edition: 2015

Cover Illustration: Sandra Waggoner | www.sandrawaggoner.com

Published by:
Sable Creek Press
PO Box 12217
Glendale, AZ 85318
www.sablecreekpress.com

A Fictional
Christian Mission Story

Journey to the Far Islands

CHAPTER 1: The Cave

THE SUN GLINTED on the bead of sweat that balanced on Rondoni's brow. He bit his lower lip. There were only two boys left to draw, and one of them was going to get the black shell.

"Rondoni. Banta." Both boys looked to the speaker. "When I say three, both of you reach in together and draw the last two shells. Understand?"

The boys nodded, neither wanting his voice to shake if he were to answer aloud.

"One ... two ... three!"

Rondoni felt his hand tremble and hoped none of the boys could see it. Together they reached into the hollow of the log and fished for the lucky shell. Rondoni's searching touch swept across a shell. He closed his clammy fingers about it and couldn't help but think that all shells felt alike no matter what color they were. With his whole heart he hoped he had not grabbed the black shell. "Please, Lord." He breathed the words to himself as he pulled his hand from the half-rotted log.

He looked across at Banta. He, too, was sweating as he held his shell tight. Rondoni watched as Banta swallowed and stared at his fisted hand. Slowly Banta eased his grip to peek inside. Laughter rippled across his face, and he heaved a sigh of relief.

Rondoni's lips tightened as he clamped his eyes shut. He didn't have to open his fingers to know he held the black shell. He felt like screaming. He wished he could throw it as far as it would go and then follow it deep into the jungle. He forced himself to open his eyes. Every boy in the clearing was looking at him. A cold shiver shook his body while the black shell seemed to burn in his fist.

"Well?" Tarkan asked.

Slowly Rondoni opened his fist. The black shell shone in the shaft of sunlight, condemning him.

"Now's the best time, Rondoni. We all saw Renogwa leave, and he hasn't come back. You go on in, and we'll holler if we see him coming this way," Tarkan urged. "Besides, if your God is as strong as you say he is, He'll take care of you."

Rondoni nodded. He wished his God had taken care of him by not letting him pull the black shell out of the rotten log. Rondoni's legs felt weak, but he forced them to stand strong. The dare had been a stupid idea, and he should never have agreed to it. Now there was no way out that would not prove he was a coward and his God was a weakling. Rondoni took a deep breath and started toward the cave.

The cave belonged to Renogwa, the trainer. He was the one who taught the boys who were lucky enough to return from their journey to the Far Islands. Renogwa taught them how to reach the Great Spirit. No one knew Renogwa's age. He didn't move as if he was old, and sometimes he seemed to appear from nowhere. His face held the crevices of age, but his one eye held the fire of life. He wore a patch over the other. Rumor explained it as a battle scar from a raging fight with the Great Spirit of the Rattituti bird. Whatever had happened, it spooked all the boys who would make the journey to the Far Islands this year.

Rondoni reached the opening of the cave and stopped. He would not look back. He could feel the eyes of every boy planted on him.

"Please, Jesus," he whispered as he stepped inside. He leaned against the cold rock wall of the cave and tried to let his eyes adjust to the darkness. A small fire had been left burning in a hollowed pit against the far side of the cave. On the rock wall above the fire was a painting of the hallowed Rattituti bird. As the flames flickered they caught the colors in the wings of the bird, making it look like they were fluttering.

Slowly Rondoni's eyes became accustomed to the light inside the yawning mountain cave. He choked on the unusual, dank smells in the cave. Rondoni couldn't place them. What if the musty odors held special powers? Along one wall were hewn ledges. Baskets and bowls sat lined up across them. Rondoni stepped closer to see what they held. Most of the bowls had various colors of crushed, dried plants. That's where the odd odors were coming from, he decided. He reached out to pick up a basket. The basket was full of feathers from the coveted Rattituti bird! No wonder Renogwa was considered such a great man. Most of the men on the island wore the headdress of the Rattituti adorned with one or two feathers, but to have all these feathers would truly be an honor. As Rondoni fingered the beautiful iridescent cranberry and indigo feathers, a claw-like hand reached out of the darkness and grasped his shoulder.

Rondoni's heart lurched to a stop, and the scream that seemed to be busting his insides couldn't find a way out. He threw the basket, and the beautiful feathers floated about the cave. Feathers lying on the cave floor gave the impression that the coveted bird had been killed. He tried to run, but the claw hand held him in place. His eyes bulged, and with each heartbeat he thought they were going to explode from his head.

"Rondoni." The quiet, gravelly voice spoke as the hand turned the boy to face the man. "So, you were the chosen one?" Renogwa spoke.

Rondoni looked up into the legend's face. Renogwa didn't have the patch that usually covered his eye. Where the eye should have been, there was only a sunken socket. A welted scar made a web-like frame around the eye socket and then slashed down the weathered cheek.

Rondoni shivered. How did Renogwa know that Rondoni had been the one who grabbed the black shell? Renogwa had left the cave, and the boys had waited to be sure the old man was a long way off before they even brought up the idea of the shells. The boy could feel his heart pounding at anyone even thinking he was the 'chosen one.' Finally, he forced his head to nod in agreement.

"You are very brave." Renogwa's one good eye held amusement.

Rondoni didn't feel brave. He felt like crying or being sick to his stomach.

"This is your time to make your journey to the Far Islands, isn't it, Rondoni?" Renogwa asked.

Again Rondoni nodded.

"I believe you are the Chosen One, Rondoni. Something inside tells me you are the One. I shall watch you closely."

Rondoni's heart sank. He didn't want to know what was inside Renogwa's mind because it didn't leave a good feeling. He sure did not like the thought of being Renogwa's Chosen One. Being watched by this man made shivers run up his spine. What had Renogwa meant by "Chosen One" anyway? Chosen for what? It could not be anything good! Rondoni felt like he was out in the middle of the ocean with a hole in his boat and sharks swimming all around.

Finally Rondoni swallowed and asked with a timid voice. "Do you want me to pick up the feathers?"

"No." Renogwa's all-knowing eye pierced deep into Rondoni. The horrid, sunken socket seemed to hold secrets ... secrets kept from Rondoni. Renogwa bent down, picked up one iridescent feather and shoved it into Rondoni's tightly curled hair. "Keep this."

Rondoni licked his lips as sweat trickled down his forehead. He had to get out of this cave. It felt like the home of something deep, dark, and dead. Rondoni wondered if Renogwa felt it, too. Was this ancient man comfortable with the feeling?

"You may go, Rondoni, but keep the feather."

"Thank you," Rondoni whispered. He slipped to the opening of the cave and edged out into the dusk. He wanted to run, but he would not. The boy felt Renogwa's single eye burn in his back as the man followed his every move.

Never! Never! Never would he let something like that happen to him again! Rondoni's thoughts thundered.

As he met the boys, they began throwing questions.

"What was it like?"

"Were there any skeletons?"

"What about cages?"

"Did it feel eerie?"

Rondoni held up his hand to quiet them. "You promised you would warn me if Renogwa was coming. Not a single one of you whispered a word of warning. I suppose you think it was a good joke!"

"Renogwa came?" asked Tarkan.

"Yes! Renogwa!" Rondoni clinched his teeth.

Banta shook his head. "We never saw him."

Slowly Rondoni peered into the eyes of his friends. "You really didn't see Renogwa coming?"

All shook their heads.

Tarkan asked, "Are you sure he was there?"

"Yes, he was there." Rondoni could still feel the cold of the cave and Renogwa's presence, but he began to wonder. If they hadn't seen him come, how did he get in the cave? Was there another opening? He had not seen one. How could have Renogwa gotten inside? Unless ... no, he would not even think it. Chills started up his back again, carrying that cold, dark dampness of the cave ... or was it Renogwa's piercing eye he felt?

"Renogwa caught you in the cave? What happened?"

"What was it like?"

The questions began again.

Rondoni had had enough. "If you want to know what it was like, go in and see for yourself!" Rondoni turned, and with a quick stride accenting each step, he headed toward home. As he stepped out of sight, he heard one of the boys. "Did you see that?" the boy whistled. "He has a Rattituti feather in his hair!"

Rondoni didn't skip a step as his thoughts raced. It had been a stupid idea, and of course he would have to be the one that drew the black shell. Just what had Renogwa meant by saying he was the Chosen One? It must be unlucky: the black-shelled one! Then to top it all off, Renogwa had said he would be watching him? Rondoni wondered if he would ever be warm again. "Please, Jesus," he whispered as he walked through the darkening jungle toward home. "Please, help me understand."

Journey to the Far Islands

CHAPTER 2: The Missionaries

"RONDONI! RONDONI!"

The boy flattened himself to the ground and hoped the movement of the tall grass did not betray him. He knew he should answer his father, but he didn't want to talk about his "journey" now.

"Rondoni!"

His father was getting closer. Rondoni slapped his eyes shut. Maybe if his father found him, the boy would look like he was asleep. He tried to keep his breathing steady. His heart seemed to be bouncing about inside of his chest. Father was getting closer, his shadow soothing the warmth of the sun where Rondoni was hiding in the grass. The boy breathed in slowly so he would not give himself away. The shade seemed to linger over Rondoni forever. Finally, a quiet swish through the grass told the boy that his father had moved on. The warm sun poured over Rondoni's body once again. Still Rondoni kept his eyes closed.

"Rondoni!"

Rondoni breathed a sigh of relief. Father was moving farther away. He counted slowly to 50 before he opened his eyes.

It wasn't that Rondoni did not like his father. In fact, he loved him. It was the dreaded journey to the Far Islands that had come between them. The boy closed his eyes and shook his head to clear his thoughts. What was he going to do?

Clouds were drifting by, and the sky was beginning to take on a pink blush just shy of evening. That was a mystery to Rondoni. His mother called it sky-blue pink. His mother was a sky-watcher. She always told him to watch the sky, for it held many mysteries. She was right, too. Rondoni thought back to a year ago when he had sat alone on the cliff side of the island and gazed upward. The cliff was where sky watchers went to be alone with the sky and discover the mysteries it held. Suddenly more noise than he had ever heard had ripped open the sky. A huge bird-like thing had hovered and then landed. With wide eyes Rondoni had stood watching as two people had crawled from an opening in the side of the loud bird thing. The spinning paddles on the top looked like canoe oars. When they had come to a halt, a deafening quiet had settled in. Two people wearing very different clothing from what Rondoni's people wore had spotted him and had headed his way. Rondoni had run.

Had God Himself sent a miracle to Rondoni's island?

"Wait!" they had called. "We won't hurt you!"

Rondoni had slid behind a tree and peeked around the wide trunk.

"Really, we won't hurt you." Because the tall man with golden hair had spoken so kindly, Rondoni had not run, but his heart had skipped a beat when the man had pulled something away from his eyes. Rondoni had watched to see if he would be another one-eyed man like Renogwa. He had been very relieved to see he had both eyes, and they were blue—like the sky.

"Please?" the lady had coaxed with such an inviting smile. She reminded him of his mother. It could have been the soft, brown curl to her hair, or the gentle welcome in her smile.

Rondoni had squinted his eyes to study the two. They wore too many clothes for Rondoni's hot, humid island ... but they had spoken just like he did.

Finally, Rondoni had slipped from behind the tree and had eased toward them. As they had sat in the tall grass and talked. Rondoni told them his name, and he asked them many things. "Who are you? Where did you come from? Why are you here?"

They had seemed amused at his questions, but they had answered every one of them.

Journey to the Far Islands

They were missionaries. The "bird-like thing" was a helicopter. They were from a very far away country called America, and they had come because God had sent them to tell Rondoni's people about Him.

Rondoni had backed away in amazement. "You know God?"

They had looked at each other and smiled. "Yes, we know God, and you can know Him, too."

"Oh." Rondoni had dropped his eyes and had looked out over the ocean waters. "You mean the journey to the Far Islands."

"No." The missionary had shaken his head. "I mean that you can personally know God right here." The missionary thumped his chest like he was pointing to his heart.

Rondoni had narrowed his eyes with a "show me" look.

The missionary had reached into his pocket and had taken out a handful of feathers beaded and braided together.

As it had dangled from the missionary's fingers, Rondoni had sat back. The feathers were not the colors of the Rattituti bird, but they were feathers. Did this man believe these feathers would take you to the coveted place beyond this life? Quietly Rondoni had whispered, "This is a *watachi*?"

The missionary had raised his brows, "*Watachi*? Necklace?" He had swung the braided string about his neck. "It is a special *watachi* which will help lead you to God."

"I don't know this bird. The colors are different. We have the Rattituti bird which will lead us beyond." Rondoni had gazed over the waters to where the Far Islands should be.

"I would be happy to show you how it works, Rondoni." The missionary picked up the first feather. It was as black as night without the moon. "Rondoni, God tells us in His book that our heart is black with sin like this feather because we don't have Him in it." The missionary had paused. "Rondoni, do you know what the word 'sin' means?"

Rondoni had shaken his head.

Journey to the Far Islands

"Sin is when you do wrong things. Things that your mother or father has told you not to do, or when you tell something that is not true, or when you hurt someone on purpose. It is even when you think something evil. That is sin. Have you ever done any of those things?"

Rondoni had dropped his head. He felt like he was standing in front of the one-eyed Renogwa, with his thoughts and feelings ripped open, revealing his naked heart. If this 'sin' were so, his entire heart was filled with this sin stuff.

"Rondoni, God already knows you are a sinner. In His book He says, 'For all have sinned and come short of the glory of God.' Now, that means because of your sin, you fall short of going to the wonderful place God named Heaven. That is where God will be found in all of His glory. There will be no sin allowed in Heaven, so the sin in your heart will claim you and condemn you to eternal separation from God.

Rondoni's heart had sunken even lower. He had heard of the wonderful, beautiful place where God lived, and he knew only a chosen few would make it there. He had searched the stars many nights, seeking the gods and hoping he would be one of those few that would complete the journey to the Far Islands, but with the load of this sin in his heart, he knew it could never be. A big tear had bulged in his eye and had slipped over the edge.

The nice missionary lady had reached over to place her hand on his shoulder.

"Rondoni," the missionary continued. "God's book tells us, 'For the wages of sin is death; but the gift of God is eternal life through Jesus Christ our Lord.' A wage is something we earn. It is something we work for and deserve in return for the work we have done. Do you understand this?"

Again Rondoni had nodded as he had thought of the headdress his own father wore. Father had earned it when he had made his journey to the Far Islands.

"It means for just being a sinner we earn death."

Journey to the Far Islands

A dull thud had fallen on Rondoni's being. It was hopeless. There would never be a way for a sinner like him to go to Heaven because his heart was full of this sin stuff like the incoming tide which spilled over the beaches because the ocean was not able to hold it all.

"But," the missionary's eyes twinkled, 'the gift of God is eternal life.' That means God has a very special gift for you, Rondoni. That gift is eternal life!"

"What?" Rondoni had whispered, afraid to hope.

"Yes, Rondoni. This is God's gift especially for you because He loves you. He knew you would never be able to earn your way into His dwelling place. In fact, God loved you so much that He paid a tremendous price for your gift. 'Through Jesus Christ our Lord.' If there was a name tag on God's gift, it would be signed: from Jesus Christ. God's Son died to give this gift to you. Rondoni, Jesus is God's only Son, and He paid the price in blood to buy this gift of eternal life for you." The missionary had fingered the feather next to the black one. It was a deep, brilliant red. "God's Son, Jesus, never sinned. He never even once committed a tiny, little sin, but He shed every single drop of His sinless blood on the cross to buy eternal life for you, me and everyone on the face of the earth. That is how much He loves us."

Chills of hope had run through Rondoni. He might really make it to this place called Heaven!

The missionary had continued. "God's Book tells us Jesus did not stay dead, but on the third day He rose from the grave. Now He is in Heaven waiting for you to call upon His name. The Bible tells us: 'For whosoever shall call upon the name of the Lord shall be saved.'"

"Missionary, you mean I can talk to God?" Rondoni had asked in wonder. "I haven't been to the Far Islands. Are you sure I can talk to God?"

The missionary had nodded.

"But what would I say?"

Journey to the Far Islands

"Well, Rondoni, you would need to tell Jesus you are a sinner, you know he is the Son of God, and you know Jesus died for you. Then you would need to ask Him to forgive you of your sins."

Rondoni had bowed his head, took a long, deep breath and stood. Suddenly, he had turned from the missionaries and had wildly run. He had run until he had felt alone with God. Straight he had stood in the tall grass with his arms tight at his sides and his hands clutched in fists. He had turned his face toward the sky and had shouted. "Jesus, Son of God, I have never been to the Far Islands, but the missionary tells me you will hear me if I call on your name. I am a sinner! I have many sins in my heart, and my heart feels heavy. My heart feels like it will split because you had to die so your blood would cover my sins." Rondoni pounded on his chest. "Please, please forgive me."

Silence had followed. Slowly Rondoni had turned and walked back to the missionaries.

Tenderly, the missionary held his *watachi* of colors to Rondoni. He stroked the next feather, one of pure white. "Jesus now lives inside of you, Rondoni. He has taken his blood, washed away all your sin, and left your heart as white as the inside of a coconut."

"Jesus is inside of me?" Rondoni had been in awe.

"Yes. Now He will teach you so you can grow strong in Him." The missionary had touched the deep green feather. "This is the color of the grass and trees on your island—the color of growing life. You have new life now, Rondoni. You are alive in Jesus, and you will grow strong in Him."

The last feather the missionary held was gold. "Jesus is the light of the world. You will never live in darkness again. You will never be separated from Jesus. When your body dies, you will go the Heaven to be with Jesus forever and ever. You will walk with Him in His light on the streets of gold."

Rondoni had talked with the missionaries until morning

Journey to the Far Islands

pink spread through the sky. He had had many questions. He had smiled when they had asked him to call them by their names, Brother Moff and Mrs. Maudie. When finally Brother Moff and Mrs. Maudie had gone, it had been with the promise of returning. As they had crawled into the helicopter, they had pressed the colorful *watachi* into Rondoni's hand and told him to watch the skies, for they would be back. Rondoni had gently slipped the *watachi* over his head to hang about his neck and had shaded his eyes when the bird-like thing—what they called the helicopter—had lifted into the sky and had swept them out of sight.

Six moons had passed, and truly Rondoni had become a sky-watcher. Finally his watching had been rewarded, and his heart seemed to clap with joy when the vibrating helicopter surged from the skies, bringing his missionaries, Brother Moff and Mrs. Maudie, his friends. He had grown to love the missionaries and all they had taught him of Jesus, God's Son. Every week they had special meeting times, and Rondoni never missed them, but few of his island people came. He learned about the God who created Heaven and earth and man. He learned of man's sin and God's forgiveness. He learned of the miracle of Jesus' touch. Rondoni's heart grew with the burden that his own family and his own people didn't know Jesus, God's Son. Often he felt as if Brother Moff and Mrs. Maudie were more his family than his own father, mother, and sister.

But now he needed answers to so many questions. He especially needed answers to questions about going to the Far Islands. His Father wanted him to go. His father was preparing him to go. Yet, somehow Rondoni felt he would be a traitor to Jesus, God's Son if he made the journey to the Far Islands.

Now as he lay in the tall grass, so glad his father had not found him, Rondoni clutched his *watachi*. He looked up into the darkening sky. This time he had put off his father by hiding in the grass. Soon he would have to give his father an answer. "Jesus," he whispered, "Son of God, please help me talk to my father. I need you to show me what to do."

A slight breeze rustled at the edge of the trees. Rondoni's heart skipped a beat as his gaze settled on a figure, half hidden. With his eyes he could not tell that it was the one-eyed Renogwa, but with his heart he knew it to be him. The mystical man had given him plenty of warning that he would be watching him. Had Renogwa seen him hide from his father? Prickly bumps crawled over Rondoni's skin. He would need Jesus, God's Son to show him what to do, and the sooner the better.

CHAPTER 3: The Presence of the Great Spirit

RONDONI ROLLED OVER and stretched. He liked the feeling of the cool grass beneath him. The sun's rays felt like warm, tickling fingers across his body. Rondoni loved sleeping outside. His father thought it would help prepare him for manhood. With a thud, Rondoni remembered what today was. Father was going to take him deep into the jungle to meet with the god of his people. Rondoni had never been there before, and if he refused to go to the Far Islands, he would never be allowed into the jungle again. He would become an outcast. Women were totally forbidden, and boys were to come once with their fathers just before embarking on their journey to the Far Islands.

Rondoni jumped up and ran inside the hut.

Mama greeted him with a wide smile. "Today, Rondoni, you make your father a proud man."

With a sinking heart Rondoni looked about the hut for his father.

"He's gone," said Mother. "Sleep would not come to him, so he rose in the night to go and seek wisdom from his god. He will be back for you when the sun rises over the tall coconut tree. You be sure and watch the sky, my son."

Rondoni's stomach rolled.

Mother gazed at him with wisdom. "It is an exciting time in a young boy's life. I'll have breakfast ready soon, so why don't you go wake up your little sister?"

Rondoni was glad for the chance to escape Mother's eyes. Sometimes he thought she could see everything he felt. He walked over to Damindio's corner and pulled the grass net aside. "Hey, Damindio, wake up. It's morning already."

Damindio pulled her eyes open and slapped a tubby little hand over a big yawn. "Rondoni?" she asked. "Are you done chewing your gum?"

"No! Today is not the day." Rondoni rolled his dark eyes. "Besides, what happened to the piece I gave you last time?"

Damindio sat up. "I lost it swimming yesterday. I dove for it all afternoon, but I couldn't find it. Probably some hungry fish ate it." Damindio pouted.

Rondoni shrugged. "It will be three more days until I can earn another piece, and then I can give you this one." He blew a huge bubble to tantalize her.

Damindio pleaded. "Couldn't we share and take turns with that piece?"

"No." Rondoni shook his head.

When the missionaries had come back to their island, they had brought new things. They had brought back wonderful, new clothing with built-in pouches called pockets. One could stash all sorts of treasures in them, but the very best thing they had introduced was bubble gum. Each time Rondoni learned a verse from God's Book, the missionaries gave him a piece of bubble gum. Rondoni chewed it faithfully and had to guard it continually from Damindio. If she got a chance, she would take it and chew it. She never minded that Rondoni had already chewed it for a whole week.

"Time to eat," Mother called as she set the steaming bowls of coconut mash on the mat they used for their table.

Rondoni sat in front of his bowl, but he wasn't very hungry.

Mother patted his shoulder. "You better eat, my son. You have a long day ahead of you."

Rondoni lifted a big spoonful to his mouth and

swallowed. His stomach swung like the monkeys did when they moved back and forth from tree to tree. "Mother, I'm not hungry." He pushed the bowl aside.

Mother understood. "It's too much excitement, isn't it, son? You go ahead, then. I'll make a big supper to celebrate tonight."

Rondoni stood and ran from the hut. He leaned against a tree. "Oh, Jesus, God's Son," he whispered to the sky. "What am I going to do?" In the silence that followed, his brown feet seemed to find the well-worn path to the missionaries all by themselves. "My friends will have the answers for me. They always do." But as he stepped into the clearing, it was quiet. No one was around. He padded up to the little hut where the missionaries lived and found a note hammered to the door post.

Gone for supplies. Back in a few days. See you then. With Christ's Love.

Rondoni's shoulders sagged as he padded back down the trail. He was on his own, and his father would be back soon. Rondoni had hidden from his father yesterday, but hiding would not work again today.

As Rondoni reached the clearing of their hut, he shaded his eyes with his hands to check the position of the sun. With a heavy heart, he kicked at a rock. There was little time before his father would return. He lay down in the tall grass and pulled the verse he was learning this week out of his pocket. "For by grace are ye saved through faith; and that not of yourselves: it is the gift of God: not of works, lest any man should boast." He said the words over and over. He slid the paper back into his pocket and slipped his hands behind his head. He was thankful for all the time Mrs. Maudie had spent teaching him to read. As he blew bubbles, he thought about the verse. "What a wonderful gift, and to think God, himself, gave it to me!"

"Rondoni!" Father's voice sliced through the quiet.

Rondoni's heart dropped like a heavy coconut hitting the ground. He whispered as he stood to meet his father. "This is it. Somehow I've got to tell my father about Jesus, and that Jesus is God's gift to cover man's sins. God does not make boys take the journey to the Far Islands to prove they are men. Please, Jesus, God's Son, help me have the strength to stand for you."

"Rondoni. Son." His father spoke with pride as he placed his hand on Rondoni's shoulder. "Today you meet our god. Today you begin to become a man."

Rondoni's insides churned. He wanted to shout, "NO!" But the words would not come out.

His father searched his boy's eyes. "I understand, son. You are so full of happiness that you cannot speak." Gently he wrapped his strong arms around his son. "I am very proud of you today. Come, son. I will take you to meet your god."

They walked in silence while cold shivers surged up Rondoni's back like the races he had run with the boys on the island. He knew he should stop and tell his father what was in his heart, but he was not brave enough.

Birds sang with a cheerfulness Rondoni could not feel as they moved swiftly down a dark trail that led them deeper into the jungle. They swatted at thirsty mosquitoes while broad, damp leaves slapped at their sweltering bodies as they wove through the foliage. Father's machete was like an extension of his arm, and Rondoni knew to stay clear of its swath.

Finally, Father stopped. "We are close now, son. We will walk in silence so we will not offend our god. Then the spirits will have freedom to come upon us."

Rondoni's eyes widened. He did not want the spirits to come upon him. He remembered being in Renogwa's cave. The thought of Renogwa's bony hand clasping his shoulder brought chills. Rondoni looked about. Was Renogwa watching now as he had promised he would do? Rondoni imagined that single, fiery eye searing deep into his chest, trying to reach his heart.

Father turned and stepped onto a new path. He stopped and gazed toward the tree tops, then knelt. He pounded his chest with his fist once, and then rose. "The spirits of our god are with us. I can feel them. Perhaps you can feel them, too." He searched Rondoni's eyes.

Yes, Rondoni could feel something, but what he felt was more like the cold, claw hand of Renogwa clutching at his heart through his chest. He wanted to flee, but his feet seemed to have a mind of their own. They kept on following Father. When at last the two came to a clearing, Rondoni's father dropped to his knees and bowed low to the ground. The center of the clearing was ruled by a huge and majestically carved statue of the Rattituti bird. It was his father's god.

Father stood and slipped his arm over Rondoni's shoulder. "Son, when you enter the presence of our god, you always bow and pay homage to him that he may receive you and your requests with a happy spirit."

Panic swept over Rondoni. He could not bow to this statue. It would be like worshipping an idol, and he knew it that was wrong. The very first of the commandments he had learned was, "Thou shalt have no other gods before me."

When his father did not require him to bow to the statue, Rondoni let out a sigh and tried to listen to his father as he continued his instruction. "Son, after your journey to the Far Islands, you will be able to come here any time you wish, and you will become a part of our ceremonies. Until then, you must give your word you will not return to this sacred place. Do you understand?"

Rondoni nodded in relief. He did not want to come back ... EVER! The very thought seemed to make his heart want to jump out of his chest.

"Your journey, Rondoni, will be long and hard. First, you will choose a log and carve your own canoe. Then you will set out with the evening tide to the Far Islands. You may take a knife, a spear and enough food for three days. That is all. When you reach the Far Islands you will need to capture the feathers of the great Rattituti bird. They are very few, and they are very hard to find. The Far Islands are the only islands where the Rattituti is found. To capture its feathers is to trap its soaring spirit, and then you will never be parted from the Rattituti's great spirit, not even when you die. The feathers will carry your spirit to be joined with the Great Spirit. When you return, Renogwa, the caller of the Great Spirit, will take you and teach you all things."

Rondoni's blood ran as cold as the cave he had been trapped in with Renogwa—a mysterious, frightening man—if he even was a man.

"Now, stand here and say no word, son." Rondoni's father turned and began a series of winding, swaying steps as he approached the statue. When he reached the circle of stones surrounding the carved bird, he paused. With a deep breath, he began dancing and chanting. Each time he made a complete circle around the stones, he sped faster until Rondoni saw only flying arms and legs. As his father rounded the front of the bird figure the last time, he froze. He faced the statue and pounded his chest. With a great gulp of air, Rondoni's father dropped to the ground and sprawled flat

Journey to the Far Islands

and still.

Silence settled like a heavy shroud. Still his father didn't move. Rondoni was scared. Should he step closer to check on him? His father had told him not to enter farther into the clearing, but what if his father was dead? Should Rondoni run to get help?

Finally, a soft breeze caressed the trees, and Rondoni watched his father's fingers move as he slowly inched back to life. He rose and wiped the sweat from his forehead. His dark skin glistened in the sunlight. He walked to Rondoni's side. "I have talked to the Great Spirit on your behalf, Son. I have asked him to lead you and guide you and to give you much courage. It is so. The Great Spirit will be with you on your journey. You will not be alone."

Rondoni's mouth dropped open. He would not be alone? Renogwa promised to watch him, and now the Great Spirit was to be with him?

Without another word his father turned and took Rondoni down a different path. As they walked, Rondoni thought about what a coward he had been. He should have told his father he wasn't going on that dreaded journey to the Far Islands. With each step Rondoni felt more and more disappointed in himself. He had been a failure to Jesus, God's Son. "What a way to repay Jesus after all He has done for me!" Rondoni mumbled as they trudged along.

When they reached the end of the trees, they met the tall grass, but Rondoni's father did not stop. Swiftly he brushed through the grass to the sandy beach. His father's eyes seemed to be searching far out over the ocean. "Son," he said, stretching his arm over the beach to point, "when the season is right, and the Great Spirit is with you, you can see the Far Islands."

Rondoni squinted and then gasped. He could see

them! He had never been able to see the Far Islands before. Why could he see them now?

"Do you see the Far Islands, Son?"

Slowly Rondoni nodded.

A proud smile spread across his father's face. "It is good! The Great Spirit is with you."

Shivers of fear chilled Rondoni. He didn't want the Great Spirit with him. He didn't even want to be close to it.

"Now I go and leave you with the Great Spirit so he may come upon you and give you the strength for your journey to the Far Islands." Before Rondoni's father left he added, "I am proud of you this day, my son."

A soft breeze whispered across Rondoni's face. He looked over his shoulder as he felt an eerie presence. If this was the Great Spirit, he did not like it. He did not want any part of it, and he sure did not want it upon him! Jesus, God's Son had never made him feel afraid and all alone like this. Rondoni squeezed his eyes shut and prayed. "Jesus, God's Son, make this spirit go away!"

Rondoni ran. He ran until he stumbled on an old tree that had fallen. It was his tree. He dropped to his knees and reached into a hollow hidden by the tall grass. Gently he pulled out the most precious thing he owned. It was his very own copy of God's Book, the one the missionary had given Rondoni so he could learn his verses. He held it close to his heart. Mrs. Maudie had been teaching him to read, and Rondoni was so thankful because it helped him learn more and more about God's Book. As he opened the book for answers, he prayed, "Dear Jesus, God's Son, forgive me for being a coward and letting you down today. Make me to be strong. Talk to me from your book. Show me how to tell my father about you and the wonderful gift you have given to me because I know you would give it to him, too."

CHAPTER 4: Out With the Tide

RONDONI BLEW another bubble and watched as the sun made tiny rainbows dance across its surface.

"For by grace are ye saved through faith; and that not of yourselves: it is the gift of God: not of works, lest any man should boast." Rondoni kept going over and over his verse. What a gift! Suddenly Rondoni grabbed God's Book and flipped to the passage. Slowly he read the verse to see if he truly understood it. "For by grace are ye saved through faith; and that not of yourselves: it is the gift of God: not of works, lest any man should boast."

Why, that is it. That is my answer for my father. God, in all His goodness is fair. He knew that if man had to work for his salvation, only the smartest or the strongest would make it. Then God would have to deal with him being proud about what he had done. Instead, God wanted man to realize what He had already done for him. God loved man enough to do for man what man could not do for himself. It wasn't about making a journey to the Far Islands and capturing the feathers from a Rattituti bird so that when you die your spirit could soar to Heaven on its wings.

"Now, I have my answer for my father," Rondoni whispered. "I just have to pray that Jesus, God's Son, will help Father understand."

———

Damindio came racing through the tall grass. She'd been looking for Rondoni all morning. She crossed her fingers. "Maybe, Rondoni will give me his bubble gum today." She missed the piece she had lost when swimming, yet she had learned a valuable lesson. The next time she would stash it somewhere while she swam. Finding her precious bubble gum on the bottom of the ocean was too hard to do.

She heard a big bubble pop before she spied Rondoni. She stopped watching a minute to see if her brother was in a good mood or not. There he was lying in the tall grass with his head propped against a big log. Damindio sucked in an excited breath. She didn't even take time to ask about the bubble gum. She turned and ran like the wind, and she did not stop. Her heart exploded with delight. She entered the clearing where their hut stood. "Father! Father!" she shouted.

Father brushed aside the woven grass that made the hut door and stepped into the brilliant sunlight.

"Oh, Father," Damindio began, "you are going to be so very, very, very happy!" Damindio slapped her chubby hand over her mouth. "I should not tell you because it should be a surprise."

Father turned his head to the side. "Oh?"

Damindio giggled and pulled her hand away from her lips. "It's Rondoni. He's picked his log to make his canoe for his journey to the Far Islands!"

A smile passed over her father's face. "Are you sure?" he asked.

Damindio nodded her head. "I saw him with my very own eyes. Come and I'll show you where."

Father whooped. "My son. He will be the first to set out for the Far Islands this year. I knew the Great Spirit had touched him. He has made me honored among men."

Father turned back to Damindio. With ease he sat her upon his shoulder. "Which way, Little One?"

Journey to the Far Islands

Damindio pointed, and Father's long, quick strides carried them through the trees and out into the lush, tall grass. When Father saw the log and his son, he sat Damindio on the ground and held his finger to his lips, signaling her to be quiet.

Without a word, Father passed through the tall grass, slipped his leg over Rondoni's log and sat beside his son.

Rondoni jumped. He was always amazed at how silently his father moved.

Father patted the log. "It is a good log you have picked to make into your canoe. It will carry you safely on your journey to the Far Islands. I am proud of you, son."

Rondoni's eyes were big. He could feel his pulse thumping his ear drums. He looked at the log. It was his log, but he used it as a place to stash his treasures and lean against while he studied his verses. He had never once thought of it as a log for his canoe.

Father gazed out over the waters. Finally, he pointed. "See that island, Rondoni?"

Rondoni was afraid to look, but he was more afraid to disobey his father. He squinted his eyes. A haunting, eerie breeze fingered his face and moved through his hair. With that breeze, the haze seemed to fade, and the island became visible. Fear clutched his voice and would not let him speak. Rondoni nodded.

"That was the island I landed on when I took my journey to the Far Islands. There were 27 boys who set out that year. It was a bad year. Only four of us came back alive."

Rondoni was in a trance. He had never heard his father talk about his journey before.

"There was a tremendous storm which lasted for days. Many were lost before they ever reached the Far Islands."

29

Journey to the Far Islands

Rondoni could see the pain in his father's face.

"Many of my friends were killed ... my brother, Kindeg, as well." Father continued. "I tried to save him, but when the wave from the depths of the ocean sucked up his canoe, it threw him into the side of mine and split his head open. I held him until there was no life left. Then I let the ocean swallow him."

Rondoni shivered. "You had a brother?"

"We were born together. Sometimes when I meet with the Great Spirit, I feel his presence."

Rondoni wished he had not asked.

"One day it will not be that we must send our sons to the Far Islands. It is said in time the Great Spirit will raise up one special son." Father sighed. "That one will carry a miracle with him, and we will no longer have to lose our sons."

Father turned from the ocean to Rondoni. He smiled and ran his hand along the side of the rough log. "It will make a good canoe, son."

Rondoni gulped. Now was the time to tell his father he was not going to make the journey to the Far Islands. Rondoni pulled the wad of gum out of his mouth and plastered it on the side of his log. He twisted the bottom of his shirt. "Father, I am not going to the Far Islands."

Father's eyes smoldered as he turned them on Rondoni.

That eerie breeze brushed against Rondoni's cheeks again, and the young boy raised his hand to wipe it away. He hated the feel of it. His father's voice was as hard as stone.

"Son, it is frightening, but I have not raised a coward. You will go, and it will be fine. You have nothing to fear. The Great Spirit is with you. I can feel it, and you can, too."

Yes, Rondoni could feel it, but he shook his head. "No, Father. You don't understand. My God does not make

Journey to the Far Islands

one go to the Far Islands. His book says, 'For by grace are ye saved through faith; it is a gift of God: not of works, lest any man should boast.' God gives going to Heaven as a gift. No one has to work for it by going to the Far Islands. Don't you see, Father?"

"If this were so, even those that do not deserve to go to the Great Spirit in Heaven would be able to go." Father set his lips in a grim line.

"That's just it, Father. No one deserves to go to Heaven. No one is as good as God." Rondoni spread his hands, pleading for his father to understand.

Father stood with his chest swelled tight. He spoke low and clear. "I do. I earned my place with the Great Spirit. I struggled to the Far Islands. I took the feathers of the Rattituti bird that my spirit might soar when I die. You cannot tell me I have not earned my place! You, Rondoni, are a coward. You are afraid to try the journey."

"Yes, I am afraid, but I have more fear of my God than of yours. My God says that I am not to bow down to any other gods, not even yours ... and I will not go!" Rondoni was unaware of the tears that flooded down his cheeks.

Father turned his back, refusing to look at his son as he spoke. "Will you make the journey even though you don't believe? Will you do this much for me?"

Rondoni could feel the anger as the sun glistened on every taut muscle in his father's back. The boy swiped his cheeks with the back of his hand. "Father, I love you, but I cannot do this thing, even for you."

Father turned and looked upon Rondoni for a long time. The sun was painting the horizon a sky-blue pink. That should have made Rondoni feel warm and safe. Instead, it felt more like the sun was setting on a part of his life that he could never relive.

Journey to the Far Islands

Astonished, Rondoni stared as tears slid over his father's hardened face.

"You are gone from me. I no longer have a son." His father bent and groaned with agony at the hurt that welled deep inside. He hefted Rondoni's log above his head and planted it on his broad shoulder as if that would make the pain go away. Then he trudged toward the water. "I shall throw this log into the waters, and as the tide pulls it into the ocean, it will carry the memory of my son. You will be no more. My son will be no more!" Slowly he strode through the tall grass toward the darkening waters of the sea.

"No!" Rondoni grabbed at the tense muscles in his father's arm.

"I have no son." He spat and moved across the warm sand to the water's edge. He lifted the log high above his head and with a groan of force, threw it into the water. He turned slowly away, his shoulders hunched as if he still carried the load. Without a single glance at Rondoni, he stepped into the tall grass.

Rondoni ran to his father and clutched his arm. "Please, Father!"

"I have no son." Rondoni's father threw him to the side and split a path through the tall grass in hurried strides, disappearing into the dense forest.

Rondoni slumped to the ground in a heap. He sobbed until he thought his guts were going to rip apart. Finally, there were no more tears, and he felt as if he were dirt on the ground.

"Rondoni?" A cold hand touched the boy's shoulder.

Rondoni knew the voice. He knew when he looked up he would see the scarred, one-eyed Renogwa. With all the courage the boy could manage, Rondoni let his gaze pierce that of Renogwa.

Journey to the Far Islands

"Follow the Great Spirit, Rondoni. You are the Chosen One." The old man turned to face the ocean waters.

Vague shouting sliced the air. Rondoni tore himself from the soil, swiped his hand across his sandy face to wipe his eyes. He had to be sure what he was seeing. Down on the beach, Damindio was yelling something about Rondoni's log getting away. With horror, Rondoni watched as Damindio ran to the water. She did not stop at the water's edge, but splashed wildly into the waves. She ran through the gentle lapping waves and swam out after the disappearing log.

"No!" Rondoni yelled.

Damindio could not hear. She reached the log and held onto it wildly as the tide pulled her farther and farther away from the shore. Rondoni yanked off his shirt and flew into the water, swimming fiercely toward his sister. As great gulps of air ripped his lungs, he reached Damindio and clutched the log.

Damindio sobbed. "I was trying to save your log."

Rondoni looked back to the shore. No one was on the beach. The two were far out into the ocean, and neither of them could swim the long distance against the tide. There would be no help.

"What are we going to do?" Damindio was trying not to panic.

Through ragged breaths Rondoni answered. "Hang on tight and pray."

Journey to the Far Islands

CHAPTER 5: Danger in the Water

THE SUN WAS SINKING now, and Rondoni thought the water looked blacker than he had ever seen. It reminded him of his heart before the missionary had come and shown him how to know Jesus, God's Son. He felt the cold, black water and remembered the warmth Jesus had brought to his heart. He thought of the gold feather which stood for Jesus, God's Son, being the light of the world which would never go out. Rondoni had that light in his heart forever. Over and over he thanked God for sending the missionaries. He wished they were with him now. They would know what to do.

Damindio sniffed. "I want Mother and Father."

Rondoni wanted them, too, but he didn't know if he would ever be able to have them again. He looked back at his island, his home. It was gone! The feeling of being alone sank deep into his bones. No one would even know where to look for them. Not a soul had been on the beach when Father had thrown the log into the ocean—except Renogwa.

Damindio whined. "I'm tired."

Rondoni slipped his arm around his sister. "Lay your head on the log and try to sleep. I'll make sure you don't fall off."

He thought of his father and the brother Rondoni had never known his father had. Father had tried to hold his own brother until he died. Could Rondoni do the same now for Damindio? This night was going to be a long one.

The cold water lapped around them. Rondoni was tired of being wet. He longed for the comfort of the tall grass. As the moon rose, it painted silver edging to the black waves. The lapping motion had rocked Damindio to sleep. What if Rondoni happened to doze? He could not, would not let himself. Damindio might slip into the water—or both of them. Without the safety of the log, they would drown.

"Dear Jesus, God's Son, please help me stay awake. It is not so much for me as it is for Damindio. She does not know you yet. She still believes in the spirit of the Rattituti Bird. If anything happened to her, she would not be with you in Heaven. Please, Jesus, God's Son, give me a chance to tell her about you and how you died for her. Please help us."

Rondoni watched the clouds make a lacy net over the face of the moon. It reminded him of the web the spirit of the Rattituti bird seemed to have woven about his life. Somehow he needed to be free of that sticky, tightening web. Finally, the sky was pink with the dawn of morning and would blend into oranges, eventually settling on blue. "Thank you, Jesus, God's Son for keeping me awake all night."

Damindio began to whimper.

"We will make it." Rondoni comforted her.

Damindio's eyes flew open as she remembered what had happened. She clutched at the log and grinned as her tummy groaned. "I'm hungry."

Rondoni was hungry, too. He had been thinking about Mother's steaming coconut mash. He sure would love a bowl now.

Damindio sighed. "I'm thirsty, too."

"Look." Rondoni put hand over hand traveling to the end of the log. He fished into the hole where he had stashed things. He had Damindio's full attention.

"Here it is."

"What?" Damindio asked.

"It's my bubble gum. It will help us not to be so thirsty." He bit the chunk in half and handed a hunk to his sister. "Now don't lose this piece to the fish," he ordered.

Damindio giggled and shoved it into her mouth. "It tastes salty. Will it still make bubbles?"

"Yep."

"Will you show me how?"

Rondoni hoped making bubbles would keep his little sister's mind off of being hungry, thirsty and out in the middle of the ocean. She learned quickly, and in no time they were having bubble contests. All morning and deep into the afternoon they laughed and played, splashing and kicking but never leaving the log. Rondoni was blowing an especially big bubble. When it popped, he waited for Damindio's giggle, but instead her eyes were wide with fright.

"What's wrong?"

Her lips moved, yet Rondoni could not understand them. She lifted her arm and pointed over his shoulder. Rondoni's blood ran as cold as the night ocean. Slowly he twisted his head about, his heart pounding like jungle drums. The fins of two sharks sliced the water. With lightning speed he helped Damindio crawl on top of the log while he tried to keep it from rolling. "Don't move," he ordered.

"What are we going to do?" Damindio wailed.

"We are going to pray." Rondoni spoke slow and steady so Damindio would not know he was afraid. He held very still so the sharks would not sense movement and hopefully swim away. He knew they could somehow smell flesh of any kind, so his chances were slim.

The sharks began to circle around their log. Damindio clamped her eyes tightly shut. Rondoni prayed with his eyes wide open. "Dear Jesus, God's Son, please keep us safe, especially Damindio. Keep me safe, too, since I have a whole lot more to tell her about you."

Damindio peeped an eye open. "They are getting

closer!"

"Hold still. If you don't, you'll roll the log and end up in the water." Rondoni barely moved his lips. "And be quiet, or they will hear you."

Dead silence followed. The sharks were inching closer now.

An awful screeching sound cut through the thick stillness. Rondoni lifted his eyes toward the sky, trying not to move his head. With squawking war cries, two birds Rondoni had never seen before began diving at the sharks. They had to be Rattituti birds. Their feathers shone indigo, vermillion, and deep purple—the same as Father's headdress. Rondoni remembered the old legend that traveled about the island. The Rattituti bird was famed to be the fiercest of all birds of prey. It was whispered around night fires that the birds would attack anything that moved, no matter the size.

The vicious birds swooped toward the sharks, aiming their razor-sharp beaks at their enemies' eyes. Water splashed, and feathers flew. The sharks sunk, only to explode from the water with their mouths wide, exposing rows of jagged teeth. The sharks thrust toward the birds, chomping only air as the birds dodged their deadly traps. A Rattituti landed and dug its claws into the top of one of the sharks. The bird hammered its beak, gouging and ripping wet hide from its prey.

The shark wailed and tossed wildly to free itself. The Rattituti had an iron grip on its foe and continued to pound the head of the shark until both sharks sank beneath the water to seek refuge. Rondoni was relieved to see the tip of a fin moving further and further away from their log.

The two birds sailed upward in victory circles until they became specks in the evening sky. As they began to drop, Rondoni hoped Damindio and he would not become the birds' next enemy. They could not dive into the ocean and escape as the sharks had done. Rondoni watched as the birds soared toward the island.

The ISLAND! It hit like a rock from a high cliff. "Damindio," he pointed, "there is one of the Far Islands. Slide down and help me kick. Maybe we can reach land."

It seemed they splashed and kicked for miles. Rondoni's legs felt as heavy as the log they pushed, yet they dare not let go. If they didn't make it to the island, they would need the log. Finally, Rondoni felt something solid beneath his feet. Hope welled up inside of him. When they reached the shore, they dragged their log out of the water and sank against it, not uttering a word for a long time. The only sound they heard was the pounding of their own breaths.

Finally, Rondoni spoke. "See, Damindio, how my God is? He sent those Rattituti birds to save us from the sharks."

Damindio thought for a moment. "How do you know it was your God? I prayed to the Great Spirit of the Rattituti bird, and Rattituti birds flew to save us."

Damindio's words tore at Rondoni's heart. He did not have an answer. He knew deep in his heart it was his God, and not the Great Spirit of his father's god that had come to their rescue. Somehow he had to explain it to his sister.

"Damindio." He rolled over resting his head on his elbow, but Damindio was asleep. A whitish salty film had dried on her skin. He should go find water, but he could not leave her here. He rolled over on his back. It was good to feel the warm sand beneath his body. As the sun sank on the horizon, he wondered about home. "Dear Jesus, God's Son, thank you. Help me know how to show You to Damindio. Now I am very tired, Jesus, God's Son. I cannot stay awake and watch anymore. Please watch over us. Good night."

Rondoni's eyelids slowly drooped to a close.

Journey to the Far Islands

CHAPTER 6: Dark Eyes in the Water

"RONDONI. RONDONI." Damindio was shaking him violently and whispering.

Rondoni pulled his eyes open, eased out a groan, and closed them again.

"Rondoni, wake up." Damindio whispered more desperately now.

Slowly Rondoni came to life. "What?"

"I hear things, Rondoni, and I keep seeing eyes out there in the tall grass," said Damindio.

Rondoni came to life. Eyes wide-open, he swung his head toward the tall grass. He, too, could see the eyes. He felt his heart pounding. He didn't even have a stick for a weapon. He should have thought to gather sticks and build a fire before falling asleep. He and Damindio couldn't shinny up a tree. To get to the closest one, they would have to run through the tall grass where all those enemy eyes stared at them.

Damindio was glued to Rondoni's back, and he could feel her heart beating right along with his. She clutched his arm, and Rondoni was amazed at her strength. "Rondoni, what are we going to do?"

"Nothing but pray."

"Nothing?" Damindio was on the edge of panic.

"Well, do you want to go find a stick or something?" he asked.

Her tears splashed Rondoni as she shook her head violently.

"Then we'll stay right here and watch and pray."

Journey to the Far Islands

Rondoni wrapped his arms about Damindio. Usually when he prayed, he closed his eyes tight, but lately he had been holding them wide-open. *"Dear Jesus, God's Son, I sure am a coward right now, but I wish you would keep that a secret from my little sister. I would be pleased if you would keep us safe through the rest of this long night, and be with Damindio. She still doesn't understand about you yet. Thank you."*

Rondoni looked up at the sky. The moon was already gone, but it would be a while before the sun showed. Damindio was breathing steadily now. He looked again to the tall grass where it seemed the blades themselves had eyes.

Damindio felt it. "Are you cold?"

Rondoni shrugged. "Maybe a little." It was easier for her to think he was cold.

She snuggled closer.

He would just have to trust Jesus, God's Son, because he really didn't know what to do. He had no weapon. If something attacked them from the tall grass, the only place to run was the ocean. They had just spent a whole night and a day there. He didn't want to do it again. There were sharks—and who knew what else.

He felt Damindio drift off into sleep. Rondoni's thoughts drifted. His father had said that someday sons wouldn't have to make the journey to the Far Islands, and that a miracle would be sent from God himself. Why couldn't his father believe it was now? Why couldn't he believe it was Jesus, God's Son, who was the miracle they all had been looking for?

Rondoni shook his head. The sky wasn't black any more, but a deep charcoal shadow. He watched as the sun slowly began to rise, putting out all the glowing eyes in the tall grass just as it puts out the twinkling stars.

He looked at Damindio. He didn't want to wake her

yet, but his stomach grabbed for attention.

Damindio jumped and clasped her brother tightly. "I heard something growl!"

Rondoni laughed. "It's okay, Damindio. It was only my stomach. I'm hungry."

"Me, too." Damindio giggled.

She rolled over and peered across the log into the tall grass. The eyes were gone. She began chomping her bubble gum. "I'm hungry and thirsty. What are we going to do?" She rubbed her belly and moaned.

Rondoni studied his sister for a long time. "We are going to have to search the island for some water and something to eat."

"No!" Damindio clutched the log. "We would have to go through all the tall grass where the eyes were last night."

Rondoni smiled. "Then you stay here while I go look."

"NO! You can't leave me." She grabbed his arm.

"Then you'll have to come with me because I'm going. We have to have food and water, or we will die."

His skin burned from the dry salt. He looked for a strong stick to use as a weapon, but he couldn't find one. Finally, he settled on a couple of good rocks.

They stood at the edge of the tall grass searching for the invisible eyes. Rock in one hand and Damindio grasping the other, Rondoni stepped into the tall grass. This was one time he didn't have to tell his sister to stay with him.

The only sound they heard as they passed through the lush grass was the swishing they themselves made. The damp grass made Rondoni even thirstier. This was like the grass on his island, and the animals ate it. He broke off a piece for Damindio and told her to chew on it.

She frowned, but when she saw him chew his piece,

she did the same. "Hey, this isn't too bad."

Rondoni chuckled. "It will do until we find something better.

Rondoni found what seemed to be a path. "Look! This should lead us to water. Cautiously he followed it, Damindio still clutching his hand.

Rondoni heard something. He froze and squeezed Damindio's hand in warning. Together they squatted down and listened. There it was again. Splash! Plop! Splash! That had to mean water. Rondoni lay his rock down and spread apart the tall grass. It was water, and the fish were jumping. "Come on, Damindio!"

They raced for the water, dove in and drank. They played, splashed and swam. Rondoni thought how good Jesus, God's Son was. When they crawled out of the water, they were hungrier than ever, but the fish were not jumping anymore. Rondoni and his sister had scared them away.

Rondoni threw his head back and looked for coconuts high in the top of the trees. "Look!" He turned to Damindio. "Ready for lunch?"

"I sure am."

Rondoni wrapped his arms and legs about the trunk and shinnied up the tree. "Look out below!" he called as he shook the tree, persuading coconuts to drop.

He and Damindio feasted until their bellies bulged. They leaned against the rock they had broken the coconut on, popped their gum in their mouths like dessert and began blowing bubbles. It felt so good to lay soaking up the sun with full tummies as they listened to the ocean waves. They had had a few rough days and nights, and they were worn out. They fell into a deep sleep.

Like thunder ripping apart the sky, roaring and snorting tore apart their dreams. Rondoni grabbed Damindio and yanked her behind a boulder. A snarling, wild boar ran into the clearing, slashing grass with his tusks. His hair bristled as foaming saliva flew from his mouth.

"Dear Jesus, God's Son," Rondoni whispered. He looked at Damindio. Her eyes were shut tight. He wished he could do the same and block everything out, but he had to take care of his little sister. "Please help me, Jesus, God's Son!" He reached down and wrapped his fingers around a good-sized rock. One well-aimed throw might take care of the wild hog, but Rondoni knew it had the hardest skull of any animal he'd ever been around. Wild hogs also had the worst temper. If he were to miss with the rock the first time, he might not get another chance.

As he drew back his arm, a squawking sound split the boar's rage. A fierce Rattituti bird dove at the wild boar, aiming for his eyes. The snarling hog tossed his head and pawed the ground, making clods of earth explode. Rondoni watched as bristly hair and brilliant feathers flew. Again and again the valiant bird dove toward its enemy. Again and again the wild boar slashed with his razor tusks. On the last dive the Rattituti struck the mark. The bird dug its claws into the head of the hog and drove its beak into the hog's eye over and over like a hammer striking a nail. The wild beast slung his head back and forth, trying to rid himself of the bird. The bird lost its grip and tumbled in the air. The wild boar caught the bird with his tusk as it plunged to the ground. He threw the bird over and over, ripping deeply into the feathered flesh and finally tossing the limp body aside. The grunting, groaning animal searched for his prey with his remaining eye. Blood poured from the socket where his eye had been gouged away. The boar rolled in victory. While throwing his head as blood and spit spewed on the ground, he trotted from the clearing. The quiet was deafening.

"Is he gone?" Damindio asked.

Rondoni nodded. He slowly stood, keeping the stone tightly clutched in his hand. It felt like a part of him now. Together they eased from behind the rock. Rondoni looked at the path the wild boar had taken and shuttered. It was their path back to the beach.

"Oh, look." Damindio knelt. There lay the Rattituti bird in the grass with its blood pooling about it. Tears welled up in her eyes. "She gave her life for us."

Rondoni's heart dropped. Now Damindio would never believe in Jesus, God's Son. He had to try to explain. "It's just an old bird." He dropped beside her. "It wasn't the bird who saved us. My God used the bird to save us."

Damindio looked at Rondoni and smiled. "I know that."

"What?" Rondoni didn't understand.

"If the Rattituti bird were the real and true god, it wouldn't have let that old, mean boar kill it," she said. "Now, how do I get Jesus, God's Son, into my heart?"

Rondoni's chest tightened. He wished he had his watachi of colored feathers with him. He had told her the story many times, but he felt a bit shaky now. "It's like I've said. You have to ask Jesus Christ into your heart, and you have to believe He died for your sins, and you have to believe He rose again. Then you have to ask forgiveness for being a sinner."

Damindio bowed her head. "Dear Jesus, God's Son, I know You are Rondoni's God. Now I want You to be mine, too. Rondoni tells me that You can forgive sins and live inside of me. Would You please do that for me? And I am sorry for my sins."

When she finished, she reached out and stroked the bright feathers of the Rattituti bird.

Journey to the Far Islands

Rondoni's eyes were alive with happiness.

The quiet hush was broken by tiny, but shrill peeping. Rondoni looked at Damindio. Together they stood and followed the noise. As the peeping grew louder, they brushed the tall grass aside and found a nest with two very hungry Rattituti babies.

"Oh!" Damindio said. "They are all alone, like us." She reached down, scooped up the two babies and cradled them in her hands. "We have to take care of them! Their mama is dead."

Rondoni nodded. Long, dark shadows were throwing themselves around. "We have to get back to the shore and build a fire before dark sets in. You carry the birds, and I'll grab a couple of coconuts."

As they stepped into the path, Rondoni picked up a sturdy stick. He didn't think it would help much if they met the wild, one-eyed boar, but it would make him feel better. With a thud, a thought hit him. The one-eyed boar and the one-eyed Renogwa shared a common battle scar. Had Renogwa lost his eye fighting the fierce Rattituti?

When they reached their log on the beach, Damindio dug a hole in the sand and filled it with grass. Gently she laid the two baby birds inside. "Now, I'll find you some worms."

"Don't go too far," Rondoni ordered. He had been gathering wood for the fire, glad his father had taught him how to build one. Maybe the fire would scare away all the eyes in the tall grass tonight—especially that one-eyed monster.

When finally the birds were fed and the fire going, they leaned against the log.

"I wonder if baby birds sleep all night?" Damindio whispered.

"I hope so." Rondoni said while keeping his eyes on

the tall grass.

As the stars began to splatter the sky, Damindio prayed. "Dear Jesus, God's Son, will you please keep us safe tonight?"

Rondoni's heart surged. Now there were two who claimed Jesus, God's Son.

CHAPTER 7: Rescued

RONDONI GROANED. The moon was only half way across the sky, and those baby birds were squawking again. He threw his arms over his ears to block out the noise, but it didn't work. Slowly he stood and stretched, glancing at the tall grass. The fire seemed to be helping because he didn't see any glowing eyes. He went over to the coconut shell and lifted the top off. He smiled at the tangled bunch of worms Damindio had collected. With quick fingers he unthreaded a plump worm and dropped it into the gaping mouth of the closest bird. He pulled his hand back as the ravenous baby tried to swallow his finger along with the wiggling worm. It was funny to watch as the bird clamped its beak closed and began stretching and twisting its scrawny neck to work the worm down.

The other baby bird lunged forward as Rondoni dangled a fat worm over its mouth. After each bird had devoured its share, they snuggled down into the grass and slept. Rondoni put the top on the coconut shell and slid down into the sand to sleep again.

When next he pulled his eyes open, Damindio was giggling. She sat dangling a dancing worm over the two wide-mouthed birds fighting for their breakfast. Rondoni had slept a long time. The sun was already shining. He slid his hand over his face to sweep the sleep away.

Damindio turned. "Good morning, Sleepy Eyes; look what I made." Proudly she held out a basket for his inspection.

Rondoni whistled. "That's really a good job." He was

surprised his little sister could even make a basket. Their mother must have spent some time working with her while his father had worked with him.

He was hungry. Maybe even hungrier than those greedy little Rattituti birds. He reached over for the last coconut, his sturdy stick and a rock. He held the coconut in place with his feet and put the point of the stick in the middle of the coconut eye. Then he whopped it with the rock. After a couple of good wallops, the stick sank deep into the shell. He pulled it out, spilling a few drops of coconut milk.

"Want a drink?" he asked Damindio.

She took the coconut and tipped it to her mouth. When she had drunk her share, she handed it to Rondoni. "I sure would like something besides coconut."

"Me, too." Rondoni sighed. "I'll sharpen my stick and maybe catch some fish today."

Damindio rubbed her belly. "Oh, that would be so good."

The birds began chirping again. Damindio put her hand to her head. "No wonder you become such giant birds. You eat all the time!"

Rondoni laughed. "And that must be why their mothers and fathers are so mean. They're grouchy from being overworked."

"I wonder if that is how our mother and father feel?" Damindio whispered. "Rondoni, do you think we will ever see them again?"

Rondoni hung his head. "Sure." How could he tell his sister that the log she had tried to save had symbolized their father throwing away his only son? If they were to get off this island, Damindio would have a family to go home to, but not him. He couldn't tell Damindio.

"When?" Damindio asked.

Journey to the Far Islands

"I don't know. I am going to head to the water hole we found yesterday and catch some fish. Are you coming, or are you staying here?"

Damindio's eyes widened. "Stay here by myself? Not a chance!" She grabbed the basket of birds and trotted to her brother.

Rondoni picked up the stick he had sharpened to a point and stepped onto the path. Damindio snuggled close behind. It didn't take long to cross the tall grass and slip into the thick jungle trees. Lush leaves slapped across Damindio's face. "Stop it," she ordered her brother.

"Don't follow so close," Rondoni snapped back.

Damindio grumbled as she left a bit more space. Another wet branch bumped the back of her neck, only this time it slid beneath her blouse. Just as Damindio started to complain to Rondoni again, the "branch" seemed to come alive.

Rondoni swirled about. His sister was dancing like his father had in the midst of the jungle before the Rattituti statue. "What are you doing?"

"SNAKE! SNAKE!" she added staccatos to her dance. It slithered about her waist and crawled out of the neck of her shirt. Damindio looked into black, beady eyes and screamed.

"That?" Rondoni chuckled. "That's only a little tree snake."

"Get it off!" Damindio yelled.

Rondoni grabbed the wiggly green thing and dropped it. Quickly, one of the baby Rattituti birds snatched the snake. The other bird stretched its scrawny neck for the opposite end. Neither would give up, each pulling an end and swallowing its prey.

Rondoni laughed. "Now you can catch snakes to add

to the babies' lunch."

"Very funny! I can still feel that monster snake crawling on me." Damindio let her bottom lip hang a bit.

A strange noise vibrated in the distance. The birds hushed and cuddled together. Damindio looked to her big brother. Rondoni tipped his head to study the sound. His mind began to race. He knew that sound. It had to be the missionaries. He grabbed Damindio. "Run! We've got to catch them!"

Rondoni flew through the trees, slapping branches and damp leaves as he shouted.

Damindio didn't care if the jungle swished about her. She was going to keep up with her brother. Together they burst from the jungle trees and sped through the tall grass and onto the sandy beach. Rondoni looked to the sky. He grabbed Damindio and began jumping and yelling. "Damindio! Damindio! It's the missionaries!"

Damindio began waving, jumping and yelling, too, but the thundering noise of the helicopter smothered their voices as it passed overhead. Slowly the helicopter lowered itself to the ground. Rondoni and Damindio raced toward them as the missionaries crawled out of the helicopter.

"Missionary, what are you doing here?" Rondoni asked.

"What are the two of you doing here?" The missionary asked.

Damindio sobbed.

Rondoni poured out their story of being caught on the ocean with only the log to save them. He told of the sharks and how the fierce Rattituti birds had saved them. He told them of the landing on the island, the eyes in the night and the horrible battle of the wild boar and the Rattituti bird. He paused, wanting badly to tell about Damindio asking

Journey to the Far Islands

Jesus, God's Son, to come into her heart, but it was really Damindio's news to tell.

The two missionaries looked at each other. "God is so good, and His timing is perfect. We had to take an extra day for repairs. Then we hit strong winds which blew us off our coarse, or we would never have been here. God knew exactly where we needed to be so we could find you."

Damindio surprised them all. "God knows everything."

The missionaries raised their eyebrows in question.

Damindio lit up. "I got Jesus, God's Son, to come into my heart. Rondoni showed me how."

The missionaries looked to Rondoni. "Praise be to the good Lord. Rondoni, what a good job you have done."

Gently the missionary lady put her arm about Damindio. "I am so happy for you. Now I can call you my sister in Christ."

Damindio furrowed her brow. "I don't understand."

The missionary lady laughed musically. "It will take time to understand. I'll tell you what we will do. How about I explain it to you on our way home? I know that is where you would like to be, and I'm sure your mother and father are worried about you."

Rondoni lowered his head. "I don't have a home anymore." With a spurt of anger he shoved away a tear that slid over the edge of his eye.

Damindio stopped. "What? Did something happen to our island?"

Softly the missionary spoke. "Rondoni, what happened?"

Rondoni told them about the horrible argument he had had with his father because he refused to make the journey to the Far Islands. Through sobs, he told of his father disowning him. Then even worse, he belted out the fact that his little sister might not have a home either because she had asked Jesus, God's Son, to come into her heart, too."

"I don't have a father?" Damindio whispered. She was on the edge of terror. "I've always had a mother and father."

The understanding face of the lady missionary looked to her husband. She wrapped her arms around Damindio. "Both of you will always be welcome in our home. We love children, and it would be wonderful to be blessed with the two of you." When she smiled, Rondoni felt again how warm and nice he had known her to be.

"Why don't we go home and check out things. Maybe your father has changed his mind," the missionary said.

Damindio pulled away in disbelief. "We can really ride in that thing?" She ran toward the machine.

The missionary's voice followed her. "Don't turn any knobs!"

Rondoni smiled. That was his sister all right. She was sad one moment and bubbly the next.

The missionary patted him on his back. "Shall we take a ride, Rondoni?"

Rondoni nodded. "Wait just a minute." He turned and ran to his log, grabbed the basket Damindio had made and shoved the birds inside. Then he picked up the coconut shell filled with worms.

The missionary raised his eyebrows but didn't say a word. Together they trotted to the helicopter and climbed aboard.

"Be sure you are strapped in tight, the missionary warned them. "We'd hate to lose one of you."

As the helicopter coughed and sputtered, the blades on top began beating the sky. Damindio's eyes sparkled when the aircraft lifted. There was so much noise that it was useless to try to talk.

The missionary lady dug into a basket and pulled out what she called "sandwiches." Rondoni thought he had never tasted anything so wonderful in his life.

The helicopter ride seemed to take a long time, but Rondoni used every second of it to calm his racing thoughts. Was he doing the right thing? Should he even go back to the island? What if he brought trouble to the missionaries or even Damindio?

The missionary broke into his thoughts. "There she is. That's our own little island."

Rondoni's heart began thumping. "Dear Jesus, God's Son, please work in my father's heart—especially for Damindio's sake."

Journey to the Far Islands

CHAPTER 8: The Chosen One

WHEN THEY LANDED, it was settled. After supper the missionary would take Damindio to her home, but Rondoni would stay until they found out how his father felt about him. Rondoni knew this was a wise choice. His heart desired to be at home with his father and mother. No one could ever take their place, yet he loved the missionaries. They were close to family because they shared Jesus, God's Son.

Rondoni took the baby Rattituti birds and climbed out of the helicopter. The minute the blades quit making noise, the baby birds began squawking. "Oh, you two!" Rondoni gently lifted one to his face. "Just give me a little time, and I'll feed you." Rondoni reached back and grabbed the coconut shell which caged the worms.

As he turned from the helicopter, Rondoni spied two men watching him. His heart sank. The dusty haired, one-eyed man was Renogwa. Rondoni shouldn't be surprised. Renogwa warned him he would be watching. Renogwa: Caller of the Great Spirit of the Rattituti Bird, and he had seen the two baby birds! Chills traveled up Rondoni's spine, sent by the piercing cold eye which seemed to sink clear to the bones.

Renogwa was the trainer of the boys who returned from the Far Islands. Rondoni thought the training would be as horrible as the journey to the Far Islands. Renogwa stood, never letting Rondoni from his sight, and fire lit his eye when it landed on the birds. Renogwa licked his lips.

Rondoni clutched the basket tighter. The birds were only half-grown babies. What could Renogwa want with them? Oh, he might raise them until they were grown and then kill them for their feathers, but not if Rondoni could help it.

Renogwa grabbed the arm of the man next to him and pointed to Rondoni. He began shouting so fast Rondoni couldn't understand him. The man beside Renogwa gaped at Rondoni then turned and sped through the trees. Renogwa stood motionless and stared at the young boy.

The missionary moved beside Rondoni. He did not take his eyes off of Renogwa, who had never had any welcome for the missionaries. Clutching Damindio's hand he said, "Come on you two. Let's get you inside the hut."

Even though Rondoni's back was turned, he could feel the piercing eye of Renogwa. Within minutes, jungle drums were pounding. The missionary crossed to where Rondoni stood at the window. "Do you understand what the drums are saying?"

Rondoni shook his head. "It's one of the things you learn after your journey to the Far Islands, but something really important has happened. That much I know."

The drums continued to beat the same message over and over again.

Damindio brought a bowl of stew. Rondoni ate while he watched, but he only paid half attention to his food. The sun sat while the moon rose. Still the drums beat. It didn't bother the Rattituti babies. They called up a squawking storm. Damindio dropped the last of the worms into the gaping beaks. "Stop being so greedy," she warned.

Rondoni continued to watch out the window. He was sure the drums had something to do with Renogwa seeing the baby Rattituti birds. As the moon rose fully overhead, letting her light open some of the shadows, Rondoni caught movement in the trees. He squinted to search the jungle. There were people gathered out there ... a lot of them.

The rhythm of the drums changed. The crowd of people swayed from the trees into the clearing of the hut. With the moon shining on them, they looked ghostly to Rondoni. Silently, Renogwa passed through the ghost people to stand in front of the missionary's hut. With the moon directly overhead, Renogwa raised his hands upward and winded a long echoing call, sending fingers of fear through Rondoni. The call bounced from tree to tree until it must have hit the heart of the jungle. When the last echo died, the drums stopped. Rondoni's heart continued the beat of the drums, and he wondered if the missionaries could hear his own heart drum.

Renogwa stepped from the dark silence. "We want the boy." His voice wasn't loud, but the silence clearly sounded the demand.

Rondoni felt all alone. What could he do? With the huge crowd of his own people out there, it would be useless to try to stay in the hut to seek protection. He had a feeling his own people were his enemy. Besides, it would probably get Damindio and his missionary friends in trouble if he refused Renogwa's demand.

Renogwa repeated louder. "We want the boy, Rondoni."

The missionary stepped to the door and spoke through a slight crack. "What do you want with Rondoni?"

"His father has come for the boy."

"Let us see his father," the missionary demanded.

"His father has rights," Renogwa threatened.

"Rondoni," the missionary turned to the boy, "you don't have to go out into the dark. It could be a trick to get you away from us."

"It could save you and Damindio," Rondoni said.

Damindio turned her head. "From Father? Rondoni, the drums are scary, but not Father."

The missionary looked to his wife. Gently she knelt before Damindio. "Sweetie, we would all feel better if it was daylight and Renogwa wasn't out there speaking for your father."

"Rondoni?"

Rondoni would know that voice anywhere. It was his father calling. Rondoni's heart leapt. Maybe Father had not thrown him away with the old log. Maybe his father had decided he did want him after all. In the still night Rondoni called, "Father?"

"Son," his father's voice shook.

That was his father all right. It made him feel at home in his heart again. "I'm here, Father."

"Come on out, son. It will be fine."

The missionary stood at the door. "You don't have to go."

Rondoni's eyes swept over all in the room. "It's a chance I'm willing to take. I think it is what Jesus, God's Son, would have me do."

Grimly, the missionary nodded as he slipped away from the door.

Still holding the basket of birds, Rondoni stepped out into the dark clearing.

Damindio started to follow, but the missionary gently motioned for her to wait.

Slowly Rondoni approached his father.

His father dropped to his knees and bent clear to the ground.

Rondoni's feet brushed the sand as he stepped to his father and knelt beside him. In the moonlight Rondoni could see tears forging down the crevices of his father's face. "What's wrong, Father?" he asked.

Father would not lift his eyes to look at his son. "Please forgive me, son. I did not know you were the Chosen One."

"What?"

Renogwa stepped forward and pulled Rondoni to his feet as the boy wondered at his strength. Renogwa took his hand with the basket of birds and raised it high. "My people," Renogwa's voice rose, "hear me. This boy, Rondoni, is the Chosen One. He is chosen of the Great Spirit. For many years it has been promised that a young son would bring a miracle to our island from the Far Islands. Tonight you witness the miracle before you. Rondoni has not only captured the spirit of the great Rattituti bird, but he has brought its very life back to our island. Because the Great Spirit has chosen

Journey to the Far Islands

Rondoni for this feat, no longer will our sons need to be sent to the Far Islands to prove their worth!"

A thundering cheer swelled from the people as they chanted. "The Chosen One has come! The Chosen One has come!"

Renogwa's voice broke through the rumbling crowd. "This Rondoni is the Chosen One. He is the one blessed with great wisdom deep in his soul. Rondoni has been chosen to lead our people!"

All people of the island dropped to the ground and knelt low. Rondoni's heart pounded in his ears. He didn't understand how Jesus, God's Son, worked things out, but he knew this was the chance God had given him. He didn't have great wisdom deep in his soul, but he did have Jesus, God's Son, there, and Jesus knew all things. Rondoni ran to the hut. "Please, missionary, I need your copy of God's Book!"

Without hesitation, the missionary thrust the Bible into Rondoni's hands. Rondoni walked to stand before his father as he hugged God's Book to his chest. "Father, I do have a miracle. It lives here in my heart. It is Jesus, God's Son. Will you let me tell you about him?"

Rondoni's father spread his arms as if to open his soul and welcome the miracle Rondoni brought.

Rondoni jumped into his father's strong arms and whispered to him. "Jesus, God's Son, will be so happy tonight!"